Dreams

This edition published by Parragon Books Ltd in 2017
and distributed by

Parragon Inc.
440 Park Avenue South, 13th Floor
New York, NY 10016
www.parragon.com

ISBN 978-1-4748-7780-0

Printed in China

Enchanted Dreams

Parragon

Bath • New York • Cologne • Melbourne • Delhi
Hong Kong • Shenzhen • Singapore

Wonderful Beginnings

There are lots of different ways to *start* a story. Finish off these first lines. Roll your "character" and "place" dice for ideas!

Once upon a time there lived . . .

Long ago, in a land far away, there was a . . .

Write a magical beginning for these two stories:

Once upon a time, there was a girl named Belle . . .

Long ago, in a land far away, there lived
a mysterious Beast . . .

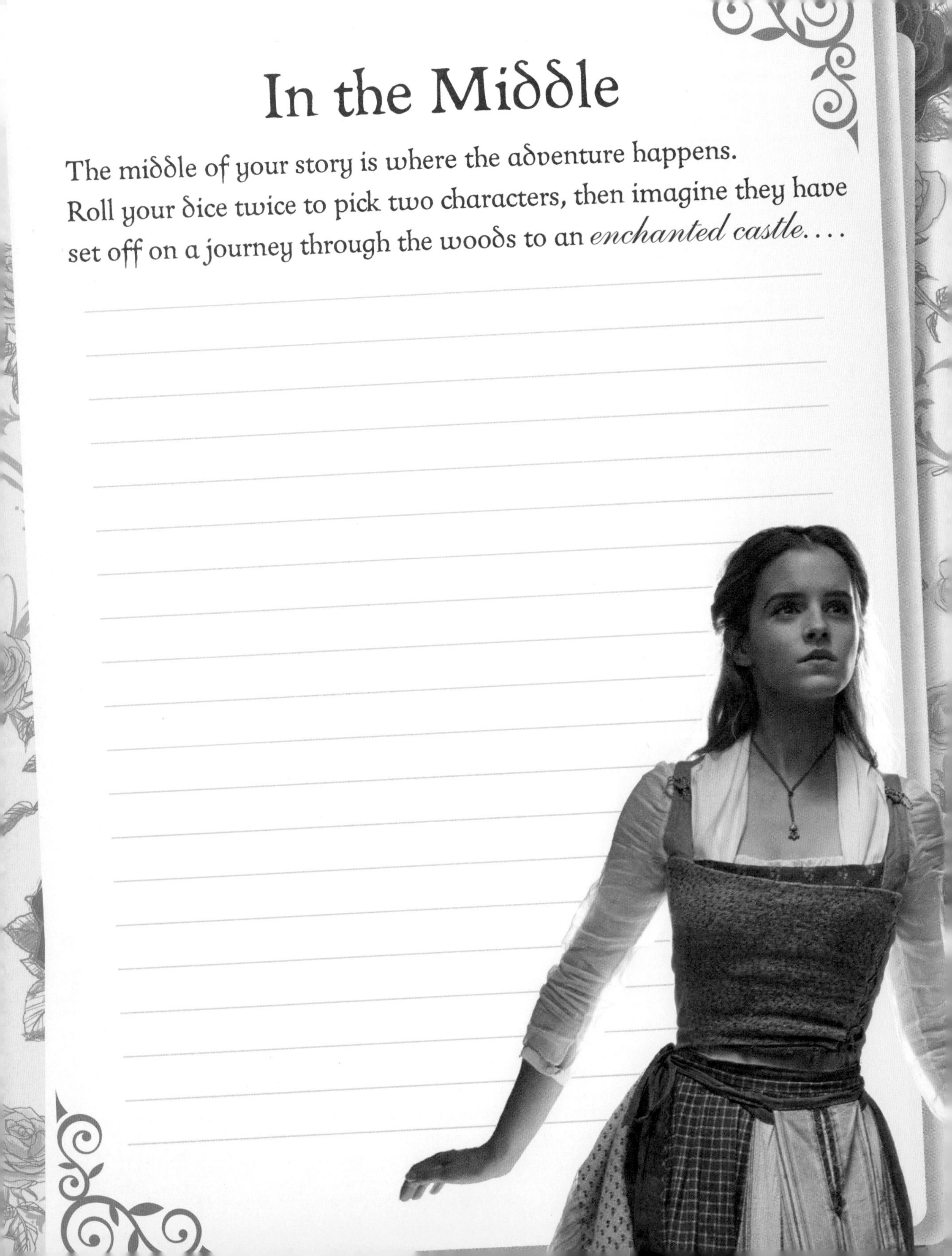

In the Middle

The middle of your story is where the adventure happens. Roll your dice twice to pick two characters, then imagine they have set off on a journey through the woods to an *enchanted castle*....

Happily-Ever-After Endings

Stories often end with a problem being solved, or a plan working out. Here are some *words* and *phrases* you can use when you're writing an ending.

Use your imagination to create a completely new ending to your favorite book. Imagine what else could have happened to the characters and bring the ending to life!

Title of favorite book:

My new ending is:

A Helping Hand

Belle has created an inventive way to do her laundry. Can you think up a new invention that would make your life easier?

What is your invention for?

What is the name of your invention?

How does your invention work?

Now draw a picture of your invention.

Don't forget to label the different parts.

Belle *and the* Beast

When you create a character, it can be helpful to write a description of them.

Here are character profiles for

the **Beast** and *Belle*

that describe a bit about who they are.

Character Profile:

NAME: *Belle*

LIVES IN:
a small village in France

BELLE IS . . .
kind, beautiful, intelligent, brave, fearless

FAVORITE HOBBY:
reading

GREATEST WISH:
to have grand adventures all over the world

GREATEST DISLIKE:
Gaston!

Character Profile:

NAME: The Beast

LIVES IN:
an enchanted castle

THE BEAST IS . . .
bad-tempered, lonely, seems cruel but is secretly kind and gentle

FAVORITE HOBBY:
spending time with Belle

GREATEST WISH:
to return to his human form

GREATEST DISLIKE:
being misunderstood

Use these pages to create *profiles* for your own characters.
You can name them, decide where they live,
and even pick their favorite hobby.

Character Profile:

NAME: ____________________

AGE: ____________________

LIVES IN: ____________________

THIS CHARACTER IS . . . ____________________

GREATEST WISH: ____________________

FAVORITE HOBBY: ____________________

GREATEST DISLIKE: ____________________

Draw a picture of your character.

Character Profile:

If you can't come up with your own characters, try using your CHARACTER DICE.

Draw a picture of your character.

NAME:

____

AGE: ______________________

LIVES IN:

____

THIS CHARACTER IS . . .

____

____

GREATEST WISH:

____

FAVORITE HOBBY:

____

GREATEST DISLIKE:

____

____

____

Character Profile:

Draw a picture of your character.

NAME: ______________________

AGE: ______________________

LIVES IN: ______________________

THIS CHARACTER IS . . . ______________________
____
____

GREATEST WISH: ______________________
____

FAVORITE HOBBY: ______________________
____

FAVORITE THING ABOUT THEMSELVES: ______________________

Character Profile:

NAME: ____________________

AGE: ____________________

LIVES IN: ____________________

THIS CHARACTER IS . . . ____________________ ____________________

GREATEST WISH: ____________________ ____________________

FAVORITE HOBBY: ____________________ ____________________

BEST FRIEND: ____________________

Draw a picture of your character.

Describing Characters

Here are some words that you can use to describe the *people* and *creatures* you may write about in your stories. Add more!

Hero Words

BRAVE
STRONG
FEARLESS

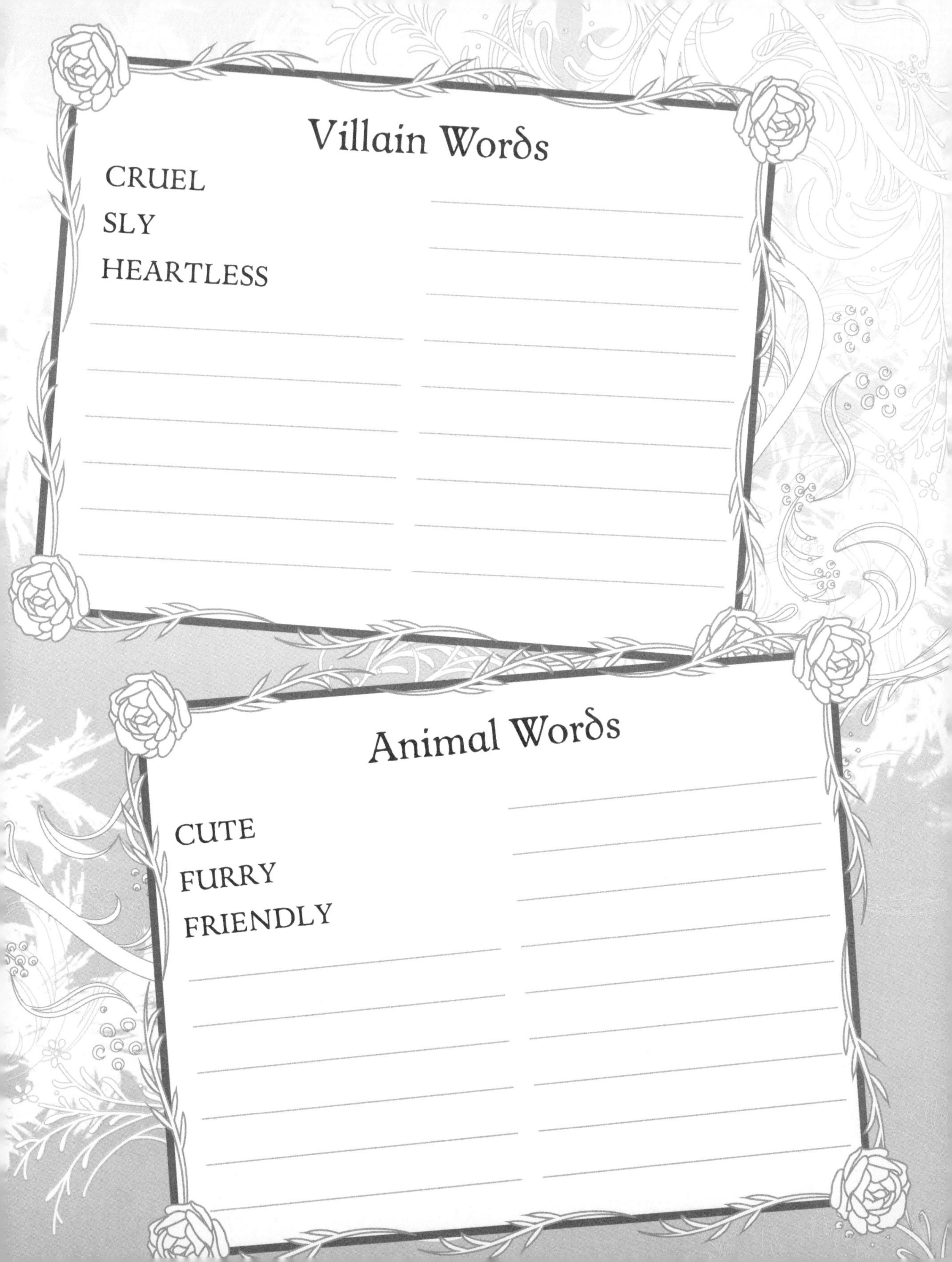
Villain Words
CRUEL
SLY
HEARTLESS
Animal Words
CUTE
FURRY
FRIENDLY

Heroes and Villains

Most stories have a hero and a villain. A hero is good, strong, and brave—such as *Belle.*

The villain is an enemy who is often selfish and mean, like Gaston.

Having heroes and villains makes any story more *exciting* to read.

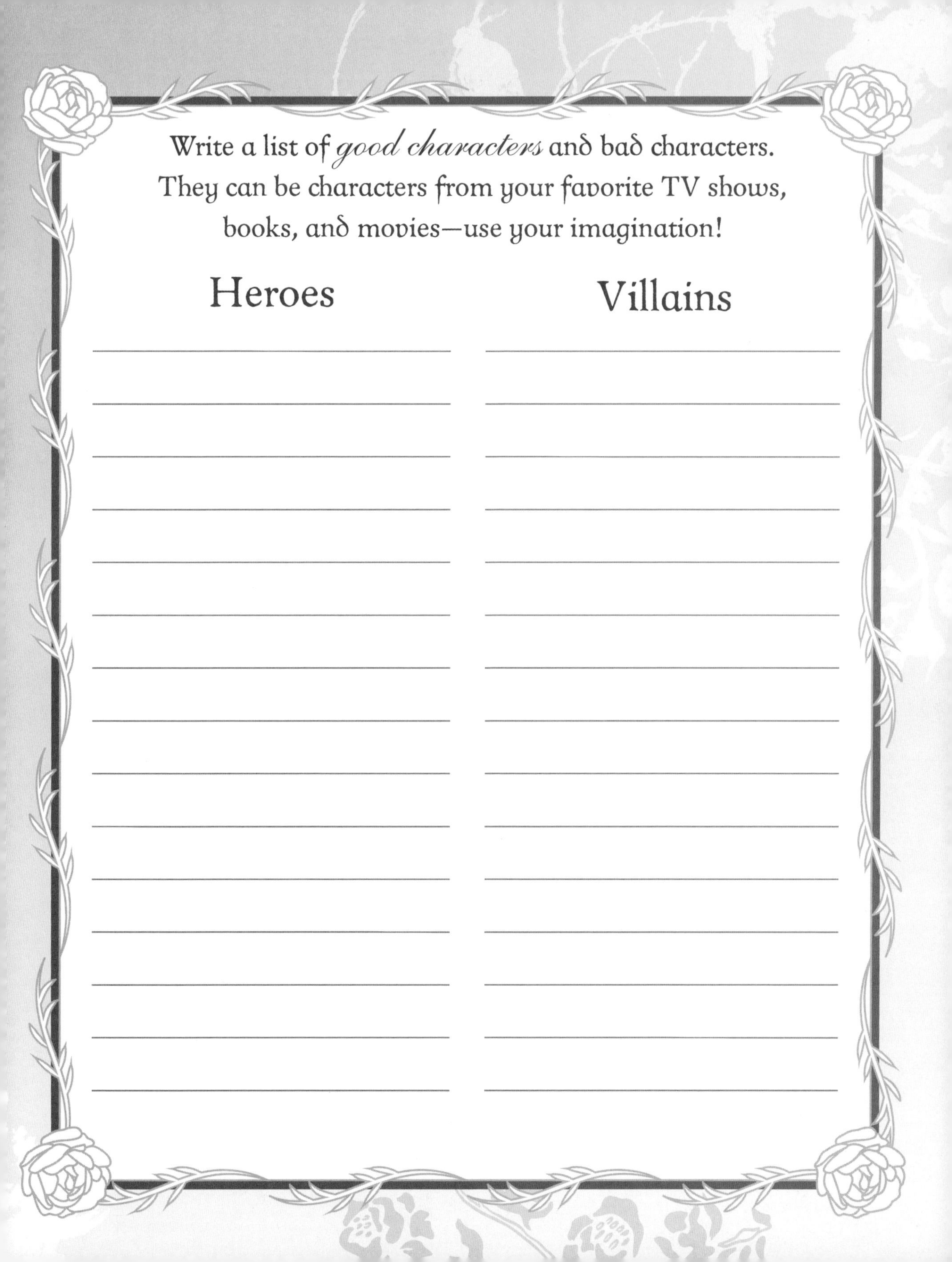

Write a list of *good characters* and bad characters. They can be characters from your favorite TV shows, books, and movies—use your imagination!

Heroes

Villains

Friend or Foe?

Sometimes it is difficult to know if a character is *good* or **evil.**

The Beast may seem scary, but deep down he's kind and gentle.

Try creating a couple of surprising characters.

Name:

Are they good or evil?

Why?

Name:

Are they good or evil?

Why?

Now write a story where your characters meet.

Turn the page to continue your story.

A Day in the Life

Belle's perfect day would involve reading lots and lots of *books!*
Imagine your perfect day. Describe it below.

I would wake up at . . .

I would go to . . .

with . . .

I would eat . . .
I would see . . .
I definitely wouldn't . . .

Creating Conversation

Imagine that you're meeting the Beast for the first time. Use the speech balloons to write the conversation you would have.

Use one color for yourself, and the other for the Beast.

Dialogue ideas:
Is the Beast happy
or angry to see you?
Is it a friendly
conversation, or
an argument?

Short Story

See if you can write a short story with a beginning, a middle, *and an end*. You can roll your story dice to help you.

Belle is walking in the woods in the *middle of the night*.

She is very cold. . . .

Be Our Guest!

All of the enchanted objects in the castle welcome *Belle* with a song.

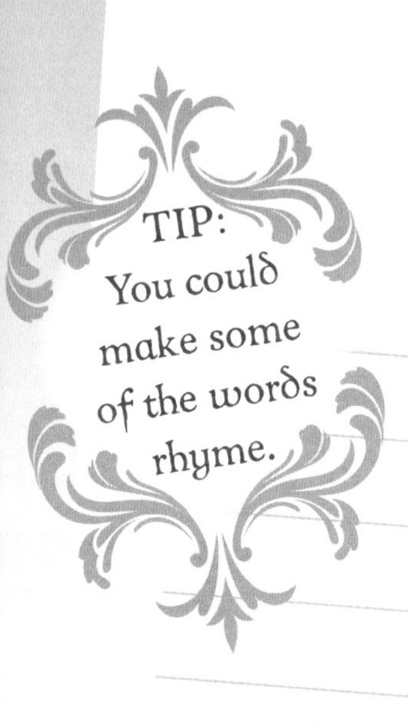

Imagine you have a *special visitor*
coming to your house for dinner.
Write a poem to welcome them.

Read your poem aloud
so you can hear how it sounds.

Love Story

LOVE STORIES can be full of drama and *excitement*. *Belle* and the Beast's love story begins with anger, but ends with love. The best love stories are about two characters that overcome problems to find true love.

Try writing your own love story on these pages.

CHARACTER 1:

CHARACTER 2:

PROBLEM TO OVERCOME:

Love story word ideas:

romance • forever • love • wish • kiss • beauty • dance • happy • dream • trust • villain • obstacle

The beginning

Turn the page to write
the middle of your story.

The middle

The end

Fairy Tale

Fairy tales like "Beauty and the Beast" are full of magic and spells. They often have a happy ending where evil is overcome. Write your own fairy tale on these pages.

HERO:

VILLAIN:

EVIL TO OVERCOME:

Fairy tale word ideas:

magical · enchanted · cursed · beautiful · wicked · potion · locket · rose · true love's kiss · knight in shining armor · happily ever after

The beginning

The middle

The end

Spooky Story

When Maurice first enters the Beast's castle, he feels scared. The dark castle is full of shadows, noises, and strange objects. Write your own spooky story about entering a strange place in the middle of the night. Try to give your readers a FRIGHT!

SPOOKY PLACE:

VISITOR:

SCARY CHARACTERS:

Spooky word ideas:

dark · haunted · shadows · creature · moon · night · creaky · mysterious · scary · creepy · shocking · eerie

The beginning

The middle

The end

Pick *and* Mix

Stories can be about ANYTHING.
Pick any *three cards* on this page and make a story out of them.

Which three cards have you chosen?

1. ______________________ 2. ______________________

3. ______________________

Now write your story here.

Once upon a time . . .

Turn the page to continue your story.

Beautiful Books

Every book needs a cover. Design your own covers here, thinking about what kind of story *might be inside*.

This cover is for a book about *love*.

This cover is for a book about a *spooky castle*.

This cover is for a book about a *terrible spell.*

This cover is for a book about a *magic mirror*.

Secret Hideaway

The library is *Belle's favorite place*. She loves to be surrounded by her books! Write about your *favorite place*. If you don't have a favorite place, then make one up!

My favorite place is . . .

I love this place because . . .

Who else has been there?

Now roll your character dice. Which friend has it landed on? Write a story about that character in your favorite place.

Turn the page to continue your story.

Friends *Forever*

Belle makes lots of friends in the Beast's castle.
The enchanted objects cheer her up with songs and music.
Write about a time when your friends made you smile!

Not everybody is *Belle's* friend. Gaston is rather cruel to her and to the people she loves. Has anybody ever done anything unkind to you? Write about your experience here.

Broken *Spells*

When *Belle* falls in love with the Beast, the spell is broken and he is transformed back into a handsome prince. *Write a story* about someone who has been put under an evil spell.

Who is your main character?

Where do they live?

Who or what will they turn into?

Why did they have a spell cast upon them?

How is the spell broken?

In a land far away, there lived . . .

Turn the page to continue your story.

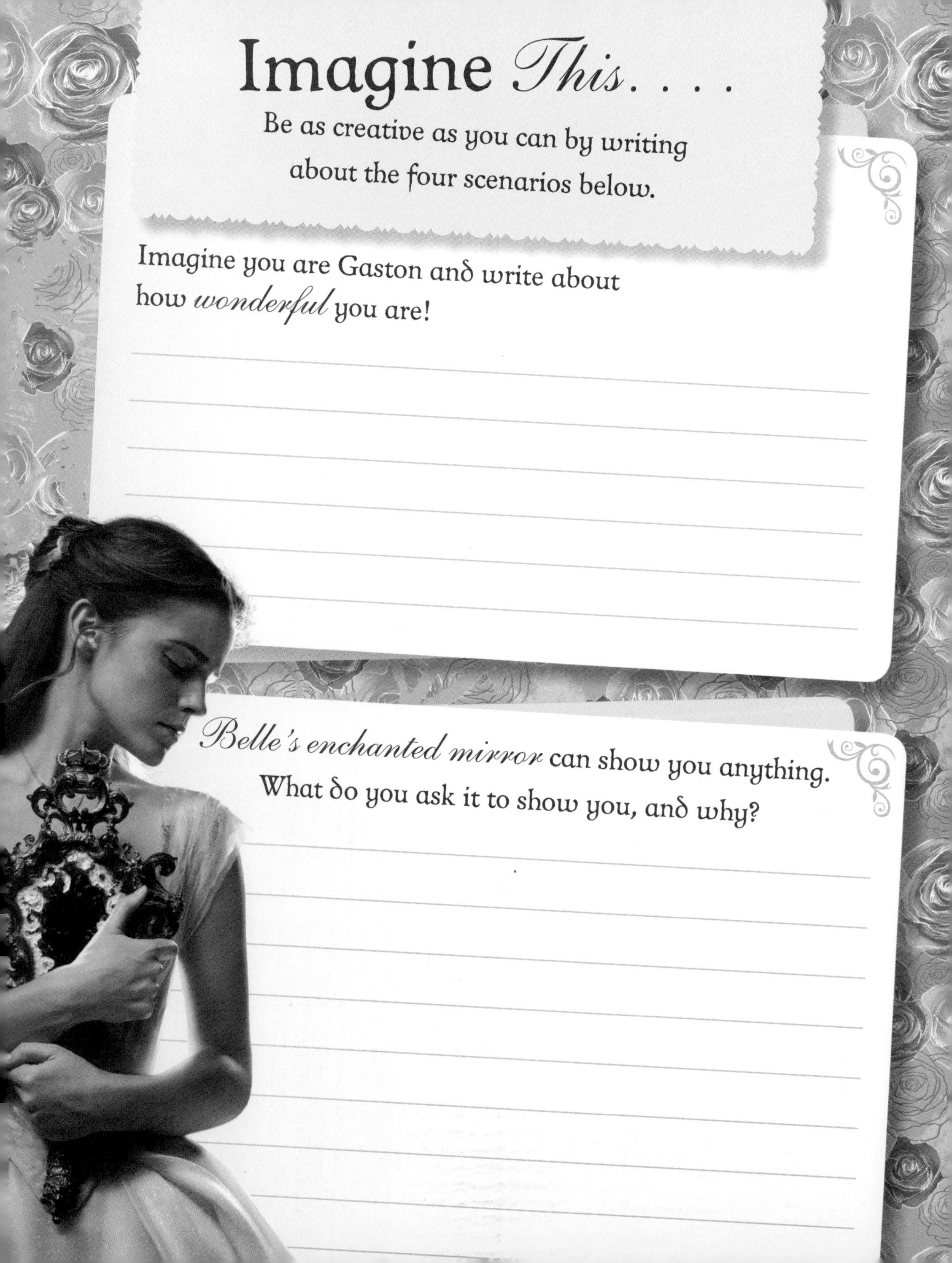

Imagine *This*. . . .

Be as creative as you can by writing about the four scenarios below.

Imagine you are Gaston and write about how *wonderful* you are!

Belle's enchanted mirror can show you anything. What do you ask it to show you, and why?

You have been invited to a ball at the Beast's castle. What will you wear? *How will you get there?*

You have been turned into a teacup. *Write about your adventures!*

An Avid Reader

Belle spends much of her day in the library reading about *everything* and *anything!* Can you remember the last two books you read? Write a review about each.

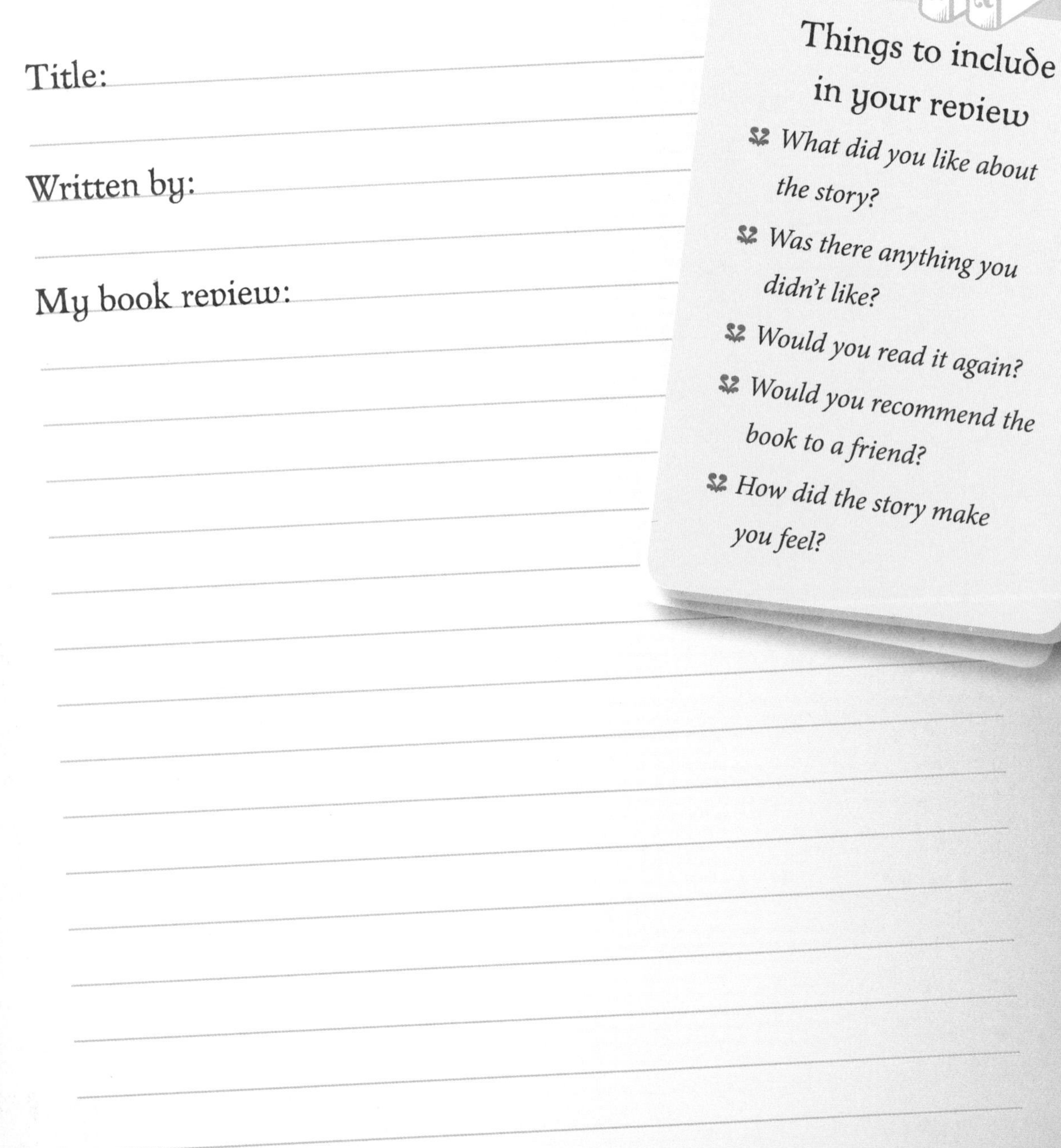

Title:

Written by:

My book review:

Castle Creation

The Beast's castle can be scary, but not all castles are scary.
Imagine that you live in a castle, and write about it.

What does your castle look like on the outside?

What does your castle look like on the inside?

Does it have gardens? If so, what is in the gardens?

Describe your bedroom.

Does your castle have any secret rooms?

Who lives in your castle?

Quick Thinking

Cogsworth and Lumiere love to talk, and their words come pouring out! Now it's your turn to think up words—fast! Set a timer for five minutes, then *write down every thought that comes into your head.*

TIP:
if you need a *starting point*, roll your story dice and start by writing about the thing, person, or place you land on.

Dreamy Days

Belle loves to daydream and imagine what the world outside the castle is like. If you could go *anywhere in the world,* where would you go, who would you go with, and what would you pack?

Now write about a real dream you have had recently.
Was it a happy dream? Was it a nightmare?

Biggest Fears

Maurice and *Belle* are afraid of the Beast when they first meet him—he certainly looks and sounds very scary!

What are you afraid of? *Write about your fears here.*

I am afraid of . . .

Because . . .

Write about a scary experience you have had.
Were you brave or did you run away?
Now imagine you have just met the Beast. *How do you feel?*

A Special Guest!

Lumiere and Cogsworth make *Belle* feel very welcome as their special guest in the castle. They show her around, *sing* to her, and make her lots of yummy food. How would you make a guest feel *special* in your home?

Who is your visitor?

What would you show them?

Would you do anything special for them?

What food and drink would you make?

Now write a story about an unwanted visitor who turns up on your doorstep in the *middle of the night*.

Turn the page to continue your story.

Dear Friend

Belle sometimes gets lonely in the Beast's castle. Can you write a letter to keep her company? Tell her a bit about yourself and your family and all the exciting things you do.

Dear Belle,

Love,

A *Magical* Ball

Imagine you are organizing a magical ball for *Belle and the Beast*. You have to-do lists to create, guest lists to make, and invitations to write. It is your job to arrange *the best ball in the land*, so be creative!

An invitation to a magical ball!

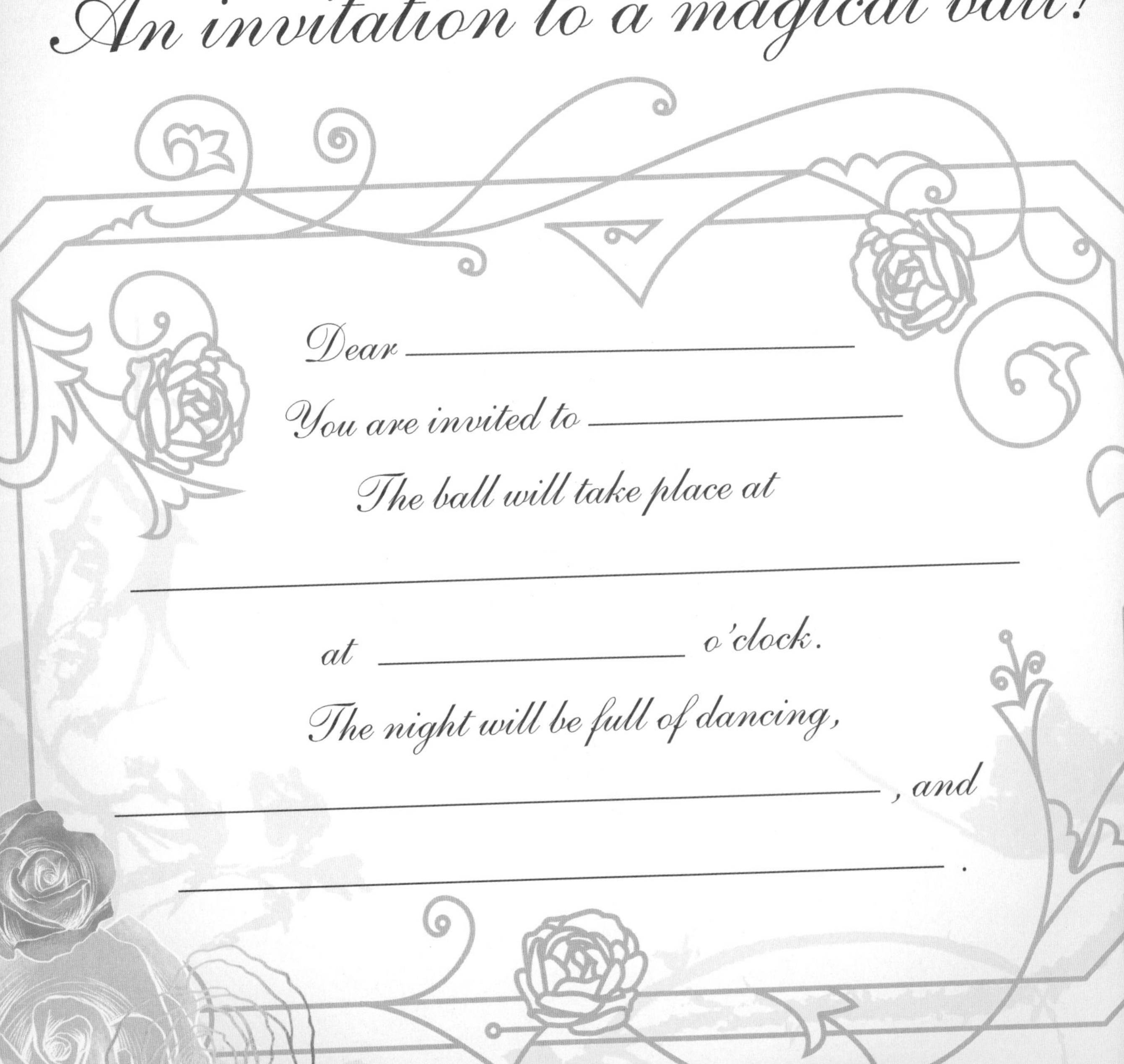

Dear ______________________

You are invited to ______________________

The ball will take place at

____

at ______________ *o'clock.*

The night will be full of dancing,

______________________________________, *and*

______________________________________.

Guest List

Belle's Diary

Keeping a diary is a great way to write down what happens in each day. It is also a secret place to share your *thoughts, wishes, worries, hopes,* and *dreams.*

Imagine you are *Belle,* locked in the castle with the Beast and the enchanted objects. Fill in this diary for the week, imagining what Belle does each day and how she is feeling.

Monday

Tuesday

Wednesday

Thursday

Friday

Saturday

Sunday

Roll the Dice!

Try writing some stories using the prompts on your dice. Roll each dice—character, place, and make-your-own—and then create a story including all of those things.

Character:

Place:

Make-your-own:

Don't forget to give it a title when it's finished.

Have fun!

Character:

Place:

Make-your-own:

Character:

Place:

Make-your-own:

Character:

Place:

Make-your-own:

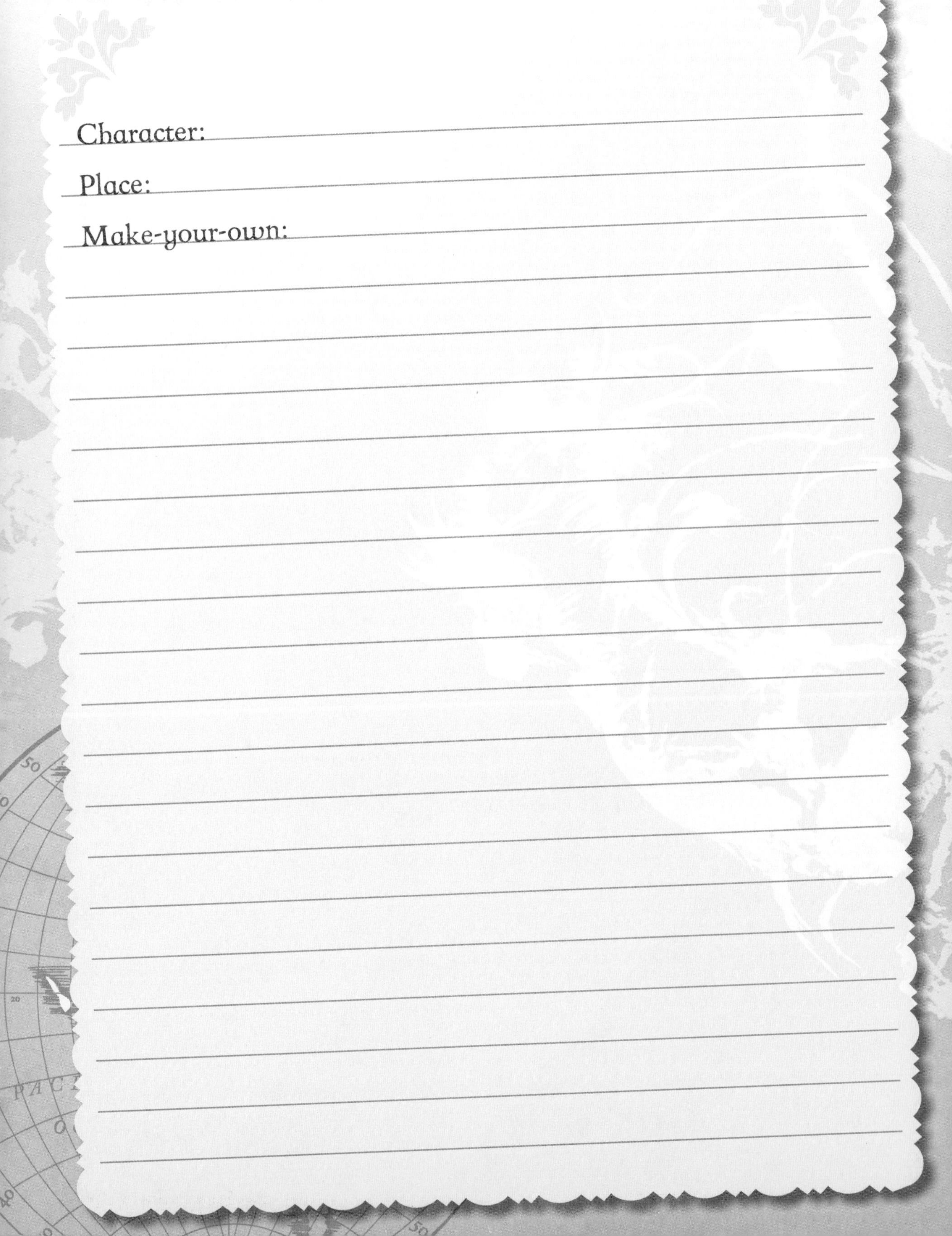

Character:

Place:

Make-your-own:

Live Your Dreams

Belle longs to travel and see more of the world outside her small home town. The Beast wants to break the spell and return to his human form. *If you had three wishes, what would they be?*

Now close your eyes and make another wish!

Sense of Place

There's more to a place than what it looks like. . . . Try thinking about the *sounds, smells,* and *feel* of the places you write about in your stories.

SOUND WORD IDEAS:

❧ silence ❧ footsteps ❧ singing ❧ shouting ❧ creaking ❧ howling ❧ snapping ❧ rustling ❧ screaming ❧

SMELL WORD IDEAS:

❧ dusty ❧ stale ❧ airy ❧ damp ❧ sweet ❧ flowery ❧ musty ❧

TOUCH WORD IDEAS:

❧ clammy ❧ cold ❧ warm ❧ dry ❧ rough ❧ smooth ❧ prickly ❧ sharp ❧

Imagine you are *inside the enchanted castle.*

What can you HEAR?

What can you SMELL?

What can you FEEL?

Now that you have set the scene, *roll the character dice* and write a short story about that character in *the castle* or *the woods*.

Belle's Books

Every story needs a title—something that suits the story and helps it stand out from the rest. Here are some famous examples.

Imagine what books are in *Belle's library*.
They can be your *favorite books*, or ones that
you have made up. Add their titles to the spines.

Enchanting Titles

Sometimes it's easier to write a story when you already know the title. Pick two titles from the list and create a short story for each.

The Quiet Village
Escape From the Castle
Belle and the Wolves
The Enchanted Rose
The Old Beggar Woman
The Curse of the Prince
The Beauty Within

Story 1

Story 2

Dear Diary

Roll your character dice and *write* about their day in the diary extract, then *draw* a picture of them below.

Date:

Dear Diary,

This morning, I . . .

Then a surprising thing happened . . .

Later on . . .

At bedtime, I . . .

Turn the page to write more diary entries. . . .

A Week in the Life

Roll your character dice again, and write about *a week in their life*.

Monday

Tuesday

Wednesday

Thursday

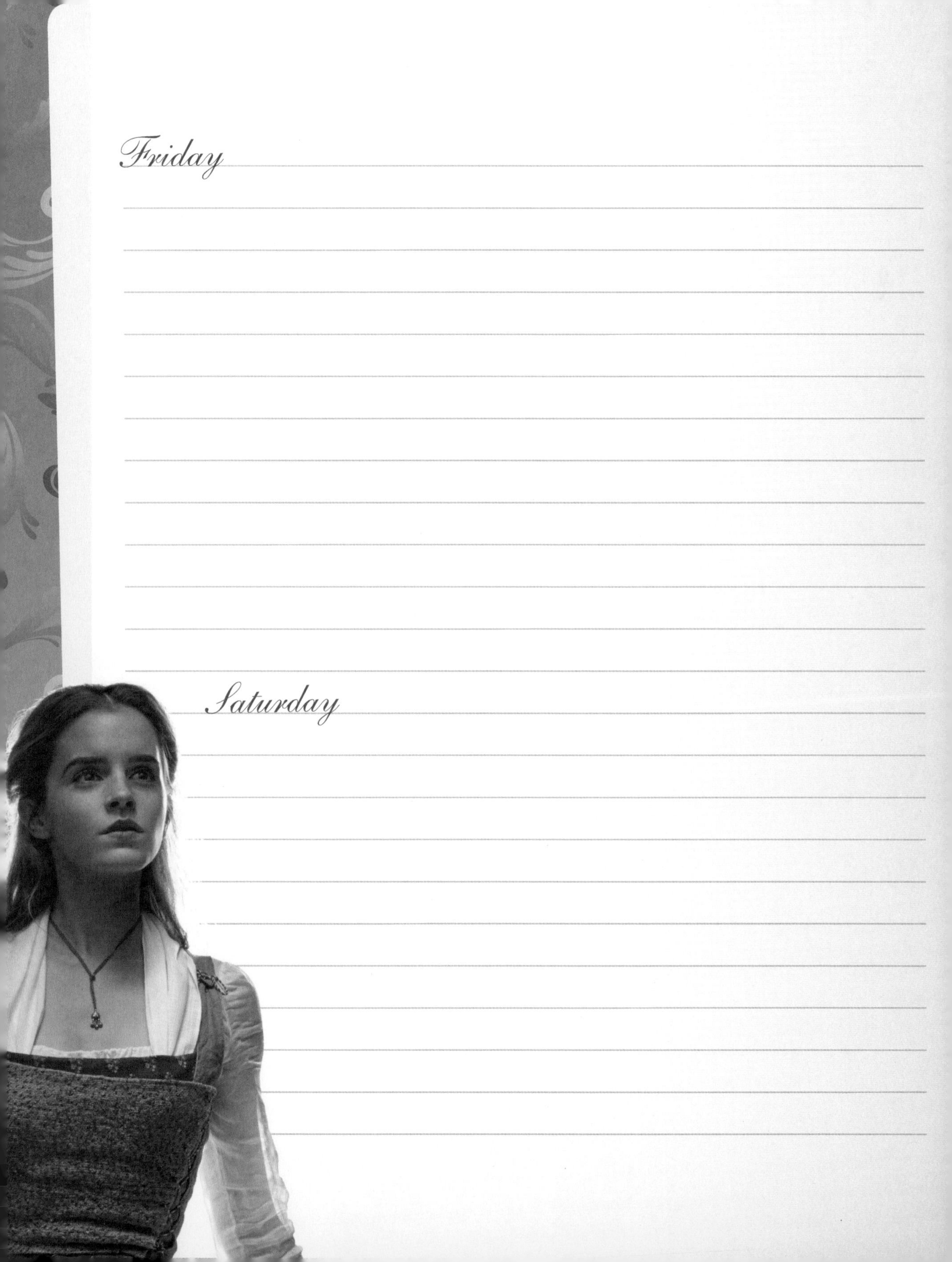

Friday

Saturday

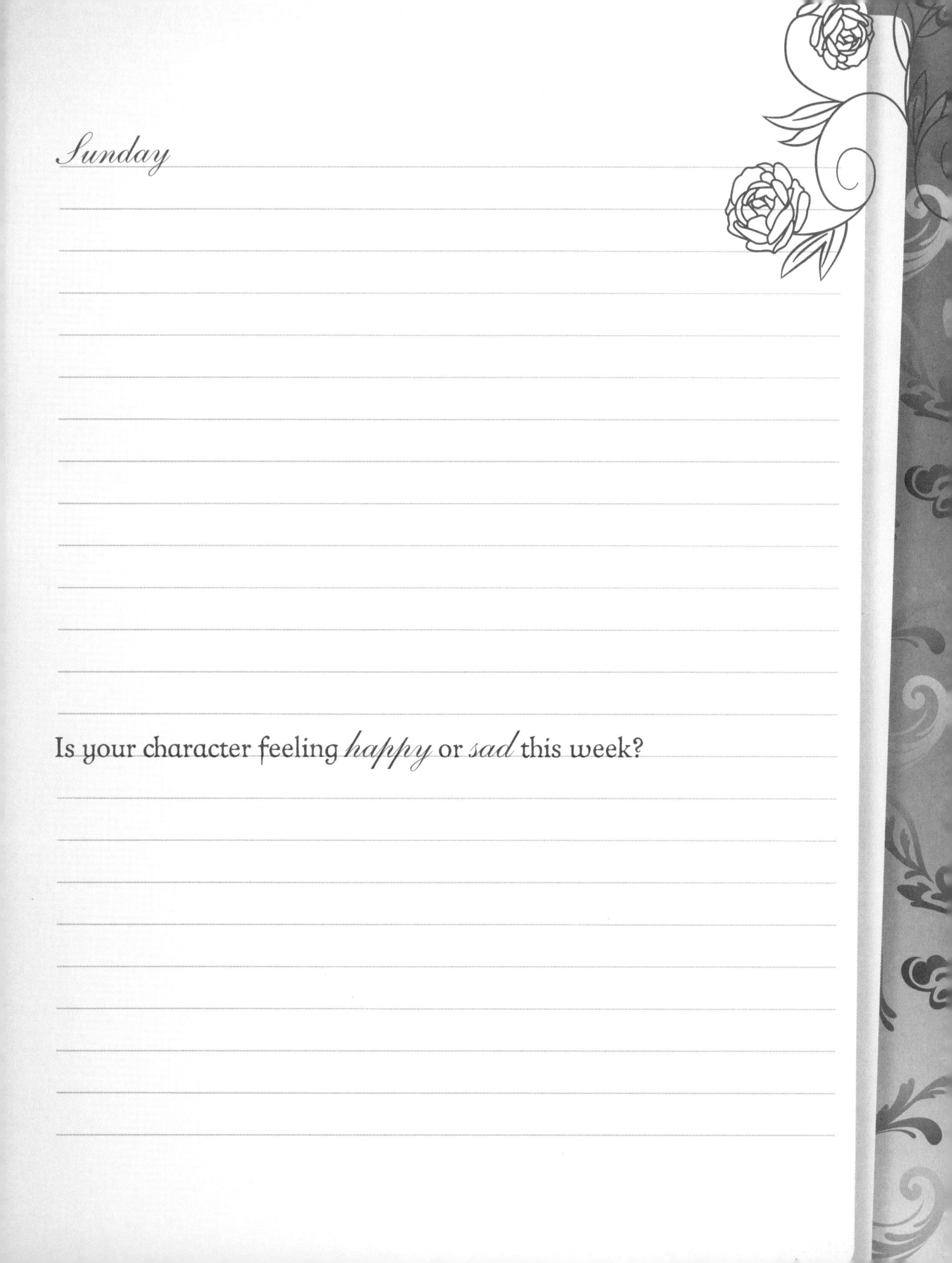

Sunday

Is your character feeling *happy* or *sad* this week?

Strictly Confidential

Now write some diary entries from Belle's point of view, describing *how she feels* about key events in her life.

The day Gaston told Belle he wanted to marry her:

Her first night at *the Beast's castle*:

When she realized she'd developed feelings for *the Beast*:

Their first kiss:

The Great Escape

Lists help you remember things you need. Imagine you are *Belle* and you want to escape from the Beast's castle. Make a list of useful things that might help you to escape.

Belle's Escape List!

Now write about *Belle's escape*. Does she escape during the day or at night? How does she get out? How far does she get? How does she feel? *Be creative!*

Mrs. Potts' Party

Mrs. Potts needs to set the table for *Belle* and the Beast's supper. Imagine your *perfect dinner party* with the *perfect guests* and *the best food*. Write about it below.

Who would you invite to your dinner party?

What would you wear?

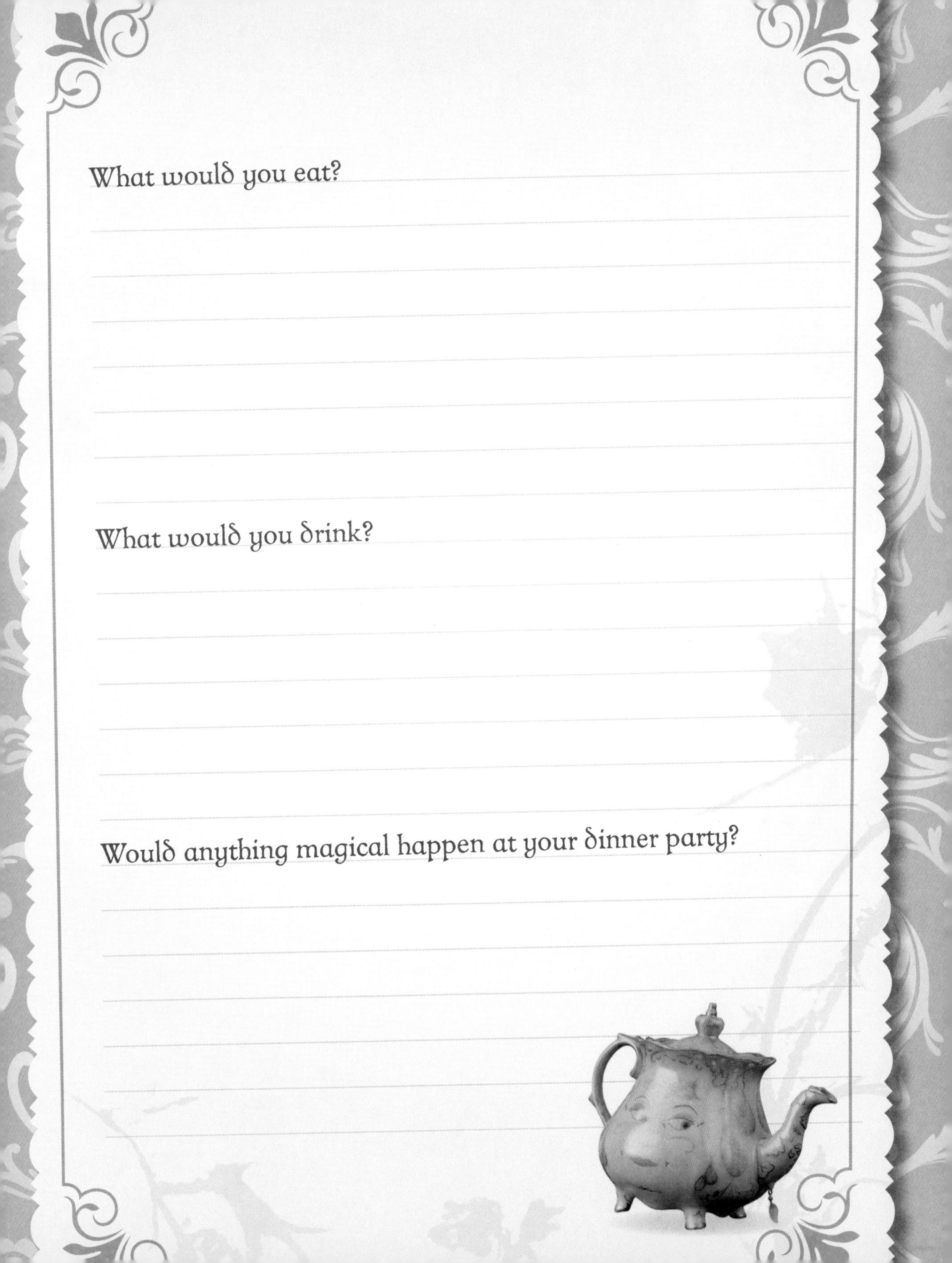

What would you eat?

What would you drink?

Would anything magical happen at your dinner party?

Strengths *and* Weaknesses

Everyone has their strengths, and possibly some weaknesses too. Here are some of *Belle's* strengths:

Strengths: *Belle is brave, thoughtful, selfless, considerate, kind, and gentle.*

Write about your own strengths here, and any weaknesses.

Strengths:

Weaknesses:

North Pole

Time of Your Life

Cogsworth is just as organized and efficient as he was before being enchanted. Write about some exciting things that have happened at different times in your life—past and present, and imagine the future, too.

My past:

My present:

My future:

Time of Their Lives

Now write about both *Belle's* and the Beast's pasts, and then imagine their future together.

Belle's past:

The Beast's past:

Their future:

So Enchanting

Try to think from the point of view of Cogsworth and Lumiere. Write about what it felt like to change into each object, and what they love and hate about their new forms.

Cogsworth

Lumiere

If you were put under a magic spell and turned into an *enchanted object*, what object would you choose to be?

I would become a . . .

Totally Quotable

Belle collects quotes from her favorite books—lines that delight and inspire her. Here are just a few, along with her scribbled thoughts.

"My hours of leisure I spent in reading the best authors, ancient and modern, being always provided with a good number of books."

Gulliver's Travels
by Jonathan Swift

Belle's notes
To me, this sounds like heaven! Time just seems to disappear when I'm in the castle library.

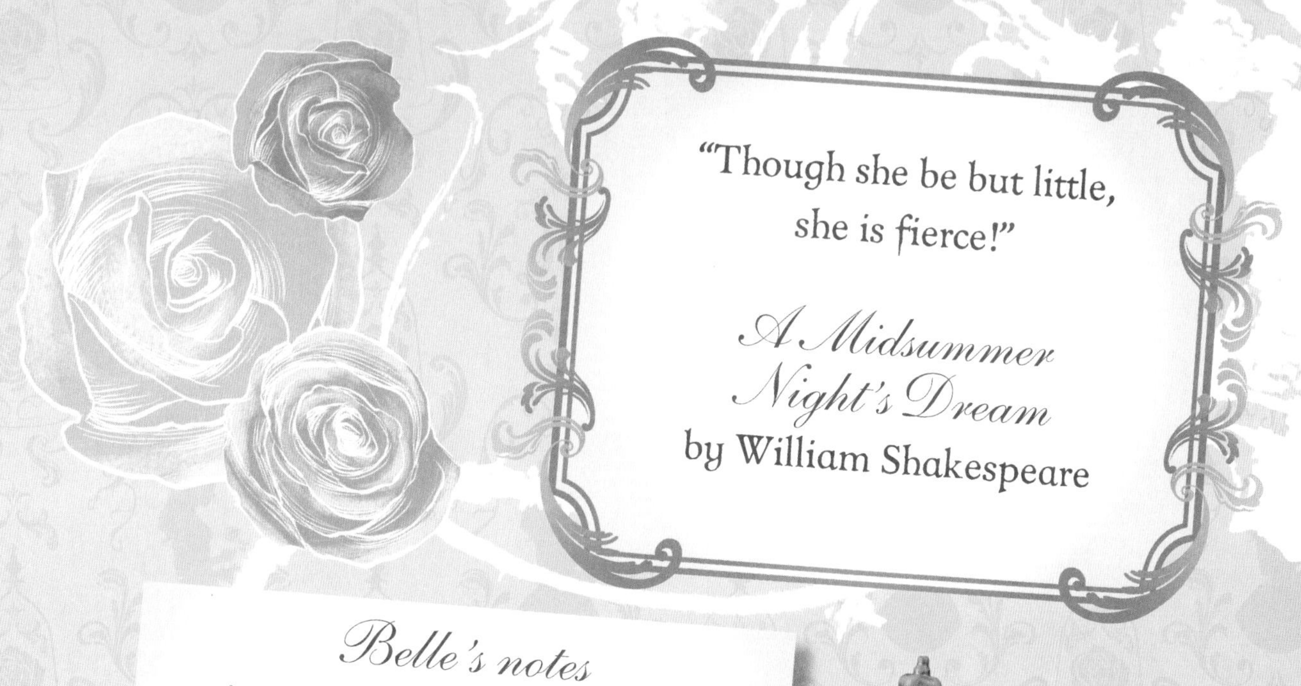

"Though she be but little,
she is fierce!"

A Midsummer Night's Dream
by William Shakespeare

Belle's notes

Shakespeare could be talking about Mrs. Potts here. She's a little teapot with a big heart, and she isn't afraid of the Beast!

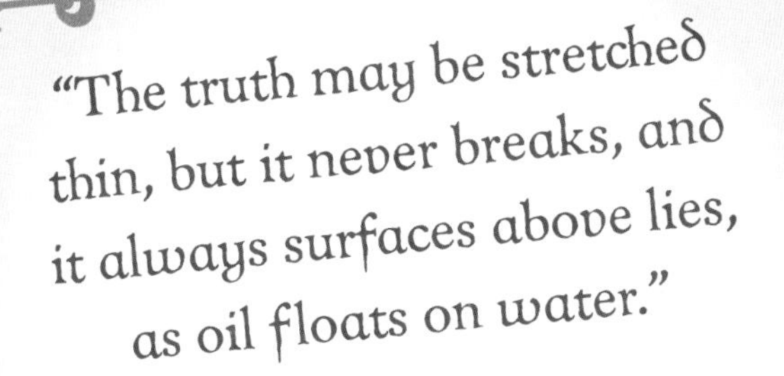

"The truth may be stretched thin, but it never breaks, and it always surfaces above lies, as oil floats on water."

Don Quixote
by Miguel de Cervantes Saavedra

Belle's notes

I feel there is a truth yet to be revealed here in the castle.... I wonder if it ever shall be?

Totally Quoteable

"People can die of mere imagination."

by Geoffrey Chaucer

Belle's notes

Thank goodness this isn't true, or I don't know what would have become of me!

"Each day my reason tells me so; but reason doesn't rule in love, you know."

by Molière

Belle's notes

This quote fascinates me, as, quite unexpectedly, I find my feelings for the Beast changing and growing. . . .

Do you have any favorite quotes?
Write them here, and note down your thoughts, too.
My thoughts
My thoughts

Light It Up

LUMIERE lights up the castle with his *flickering candles and bright personality*. Describe being in a dark room, and what surprises you discover when the lights come on. . . .

Family Fun

Belle loves her father, Maurice, dearly.
Tell your *favorite tales* about your family here.

Holiday traditions:

Funniest family moment:

PACIF
OCE

An exciting vacation:

Feeling Funny

The Beast often struggles to conceal his emotions. Describe some of the things that make you feel . . .

Angry:

Afraid:

The Next Big Thing

MAURICE, *Belle's father*, makes music boxes that represent exotic places around the world. Imagine you are an inventor and are being interviewed by a journalist about your latest creation!

Write a newspaper article about your invention, to let the people know what it's called and what it does.

Title of the article

Draw a picture here

Write the article here
Written by

Home *Sweet Home*

Belle felt afraid when she first set foot inside the Beast's castle, but she soon made friends with its residents and began to feel at home. Tell Belle all about your home.

What it looks like on the outside:

Your favorite room:

The garden:

Where your family spends most of their time:

Mixed-Up *Magic*

Long ago, an *enchantress* put a spell on the castle and everyone who lived there. Try to conjure up your own spell, and describe what will happen when the magical words are recited.

Name of spell:

Words of spell:

Effects of spell:

Dream Dinners

Belle's hosts at the castle prepared a fabulous *welcome meal* for her. Imagine and describe in delicious detail the food your characters would feast on at these *special occasions*.

A birthday celebration
A village fair

About the Author

Imagine you're a world-famous author. (Maybe one day you will be!)
Tell your fans a little bit about yourself here.

My full name is:

I live with:

My favorite book is:

My best friend's name is:

My biggest ambition is:
My signature looks like this:
My first memory is:
My favorite thing about myself is:
I feel happiest when:

Credits

This book features stories, poems, rhymes, ideas, descriptions, lists, letters, and diary entries *written by:*

---

write your name here

Use this page to *practice your signature* for when you are a famous author.

Lots of books have a picture of the author in the back.

Draw or paste a picture of yourself here.

Use these pages to write notes and stories,
doodle characters, scribble songs, or create poems. . . .

Use them however you like!

Inspire

Imagine

Create

Believe

Word Bank

Whenever you come across a word that's exciting or new, write it down here—with its meaning—so you don't forget it! Then, when you come to write your stories, you will have a bank of fantastic words to use.

GLISTENING: shining with a sparkling light